Weenie

featuring Frank & Beans

THE PANCAKE PROBLEM

WRITTEN BY

Maureen Fergus

ILLUSTRATED BY

Alexandra Bye

tundra

FOR STEVEN: YOU ARE MY BROTHER. — MF

FOR CHIP. THANKS FOR TEACHING ME NOT TO TAKE LIFE
SO SERIOUSLY. CHEERS TO PANCAKES, MEATLOAF
AND OUR GOOFY DOG. — AB

Tundra Books, an imprint of Tundra Book Group,
a division of Penguin Random House of Canada Limited

Library and Archives Canada Cataloguing in Publication

Title: The pancake problem / Maureen Fergus ; Alexandra Bye, illustrator.
Names: Fergus, Maureen, author. | Bye, Alexandra, illustrator.
Description: Series statement: Weenie featuring Frank and Beans
Identifiers: Canadiana (print) 20210353066 | Canadiana (ebook) 20210353090 |
ISBN 9780735267947 (hardcover) | ISBN 9780735267954 (EPUB)
Subjects: LCGFT: Graphic novels.
Classification: LCC PN6733.F47 P36 2022 | DDC j741.5/971—dc23

Published simultaneously in the United States of America by
Tundra Books of Northern New York, an imprint of Tundra Book Group,
a division of Penguin Random House of Canada Limited

Library of Congress Control Number: 2021949357

Edited by Samantha Swenson
Designed by John Martz
The artwork in this book was rendered with Photoshop and dog hair.
The text was set in DigitalStrip BB.

Printed in China

www.penguinrandomhouse.ca

1   2   3   4   5   27   26   25   24   23

Penguin
Random House
tundra   TUNDRA BOOKS

THE PANCAKE PROBLEM

Chapter 1
BOB'S #2 RULE

HELLO! I'M SO GLAD TO SEE YOU!

AREN'T YOU EVEN GOING TO SAY HELLO BACK TO ME?

SHHHH!

NOT SO LOUD! YOU'LL WAKE UP FRANK AND BEANS.

FRANK

BEANS

A VERY WEENIE DEFINITION OF THE WORD **FAMISHED**:

famished / fam·ished / *adjective*
When a wiener dog is SO HUNGRY that if he doesn't get fed immediately, he will destroy and eat the couch cushions.*

*Actually, he will probably do that anyway.

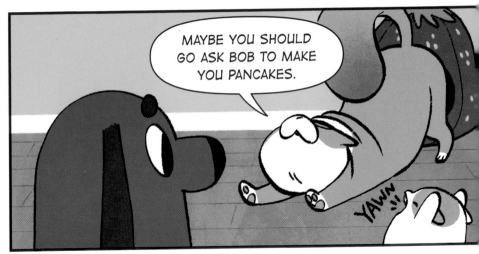

BOB'S #2 RULE

ALWAYS FOLLOW BOB'S NUMBER ONE RULE.

Chapter 2
The MONSTER

BAD NEWS! BOB ISN'T UP HERE! THERE IS ONLY A BOB-SHAPED LUMP UNDER THE COVERS.

DOES THE LUMP **SOUND** LIKE BOB?

YES.

DOES THE LUMP **SMELL** LIKE BOB?

Chapter 3

The SUPERSONIC PANCAKE MAKER

I CAN'T BELIEVE BOB REFUSED TO GET UP AND MAKE ME PANCAKES EVEN AFTER I EXPLAINED THAT I AM FAMISHED.

DID HE THANK YOU FOR SAVING HIM FROM THE MONSTER?

NO!

A SHOCKING FACT ABOUT BOB

HE IS SOMETIMES GRUMPY WHEN HUNGRY WIENER DOGS WAKE HIM UP AT THE CRACK OF DAWN.

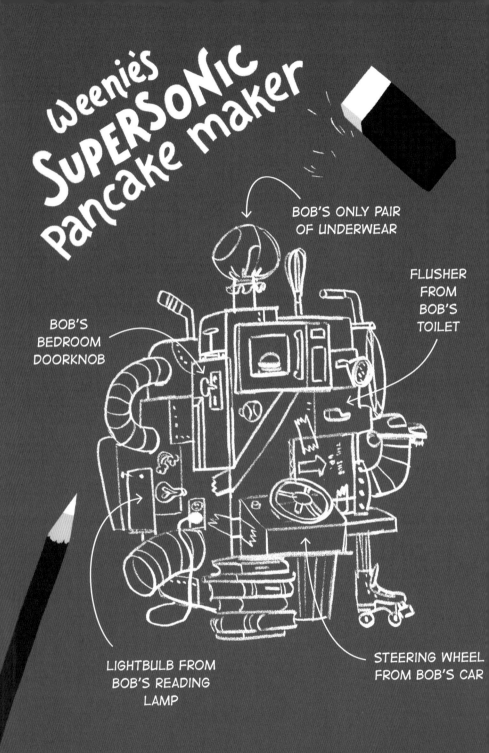

THAT'S AMAZING! I DIDN'T KNOW WIENER DOGS COULD INVENT THINGS.

IT IS A WELL-KNOWN FACT THAT MANY FAMOUS INVENTORS WERE WIENER DOGS.

THAT IS NOT TRUE.

IT IS DEFINITELY TRUE.

A Partial list of FAMOUS INVENTORS who were WIENER DOGS

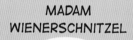

MADAM WIENERSCHNITZEL

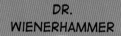

DR. WIENERHAMMER

ALBERT WIENERSTEIN

INVENTED THE ALL-YOU-CAN-EAT BREAKFAST SAUSAGE BUFFET.

INVENTED EXTRA-SMELLY, SOGGY CHEW TOYS.

INVENTED MEATLOAF.

I DON'T THINK SO, EITHER! OH, THIS IS THE MOST DISAPPOINTING THING THAT HAS EVER HAPPENED TO ANY WIENER DOG EVER! BOOHOOHOO BOOHOOHOO —

HAVE YOU TRIED THIS BUTTON?

POP

DID IT WORK?

NOT EXACTLY . . .

YOUR INVENTION DIDN'T MAKE A PANCAKE, WEENIE. IT MADE A BRUSSELS SPROUT!

QUICK, WEENIE! HIT THE OFF SWITCH!

I CAN'T! I DIDN'T INVENT AN OFF SWITCH!

Chapter **4**

A **BIG STINKY** Problem

WHAT ARE WE GOING TO DO WITH ALL THESE BRUSSELS SPROUTS?

DON'T WORRY, BEANS. I HAVE A PLAN!

WHAT IS IT?

I WILL GIVE YOU THREE HINTS ...

WEENIE'S 3 HINTS

1 IT INVOLVES ME CHEWING, SWALLOWING AND BURPING.

2 IT IS MY FAVORITE THING TO DO IN THE WHOLE WORLD.

3 IT IS SOMETHING I SOMETIMES ACCIDENTALLY DO TO BOB'S MOST PRIZED POSSESSIONS.

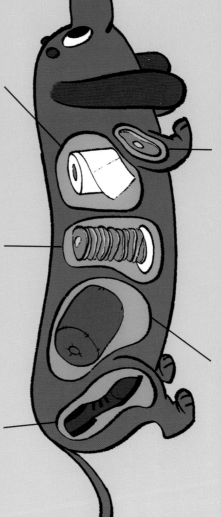

A Medical Miracle:
WIENER DOG STOMACHS

BOB'S FAVORITE SHOES STOMACH

MAIN PANCAKE STOMACH

TOILET PAPER STOMACH

COUCH CUSHION STOMACH

EXTRA PANCAKE STOMACH

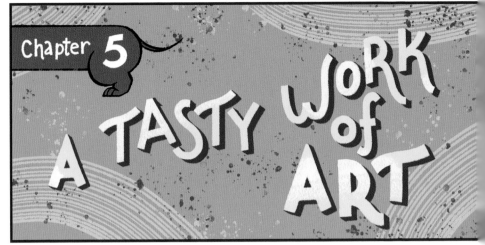

Chapter 5
A TASTY WORK of ART

THAT WAS A CLOSE ONE!

WHAT ARE YOU TALKING ABOUT, WEENIE?

WE ALMOST SOLD OUR BRUSSELS SPROUTS TO SOMEONE WHO DOESN'T LIKE SMOOCHES.

CAN I HELP YOU?

HELLO. I AM A FAMOUS ARTIST. I WOULD LIKE TO SELL A WORK OF ART TO YOUR ART GALLERY.

WONDERFUL! WHAT IS IT CALLED?

HUMONGOUS PILE OF BRUSSELS SPROUTS

Chapter 6

WEENIE'S #1 RULE

WHO COULD HAVE KNOWN THAT EATING *HUMONGOUS PILE OF PANCAKES* WOULD UPSET THE GALLERY OWNER AND GIVE ME A TUMMY ACHE?

ME! I COULD HAVE KNOWN! I *DID* KNOW!

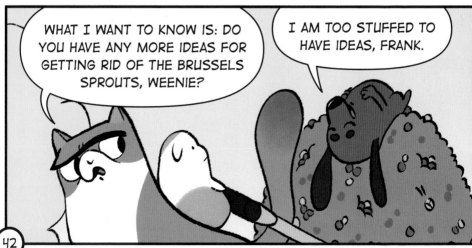

WHAT I WANT TO KNOW IS: DO YOU HAVE ANY MORE IDEAS FOR GETTING RID OF THE BRUSSELS SPROUTS, WEENIE?

I AM TOO STUFFED TO HAVE IDEAS, FRANK.